The
Littles
and Their Amazing
New Friend

The
Littles
and Their Amazing
New Friend

by **John Peterson**
Pictures by **Roberta Carter Clark**
Cover illustration by **Jacqueline Rogers**

A
LITTLE APPLE
PAPERBACK

SCHOLASTIC INC.
New York   Toronto   London   Auckland   Sydney
Mexico City   New Delhi   Hong Kong

ISBN 0-590-87612-0

12 11 10 9 8 7 6 5 4   9/9 0 1 2 3 4/0

Printed in the U.S.A.   40

First Scholastic printing, March 1999

To the amazing Beppy!

With special thanks to
Holly

COUSIN DINKY LITTLE was on the Biggs' roof doing the final testing of a hot-air balloon. Ten-year-old Tom Little and his uncle Nick were watching him as he worked. Tom had found the huge red rubber balloon in Henry Bigg's wastebasket and had given it to his cousin, an adventurer and glider pilot.

"You were right to think I needed this balloon, Tom," said Dinky. "I've been wanting a big one like this for some time. If everything goes right I'll be able to fly our family to the city on Thanksgiving to have dinner with our friends the Library Tinies. But first I have to see if Grandpa's stove-pump really works."

Grandpa Amos Little, the family's patriarch, explorer, and inventor, had used his "noodle," as he called it, to invent the stove-pump that could blow hot air steadily into

1

the balloon. "Hot air rises," explained Cousin Dinky, "so the balloon should go up in the air when a valve is open and down when it is closed. We'll find out pretty soon if it works."

The Littles were tiny people who lived in an apartment in the walls of a big house owned by Mr. George W. Bigg, a regular-sized person. The Bigg family had no idea that the tiny Littles were living in their house. The ten members of the tiny family stayed out of sight, made very little noise, and always put their trash in the garbage-disposal hole in the kitchen sink so as not to leave a telltale mess anywhere.

The Littles called themselves House Tinies. They were not just small, they were *very, very* tiny. The tallest Little and the father of the family, Mr. William T. Little, was only six inches tall. The smallest Little, Baby Betsy, slept in a matchbox.

UNCLE NICK

UNCLE PET

Except for being tiny, the Littles were very much like regular-sized people, with one amazing but unimportant physical difference: The Littles and all the tiny people of the Big Valley had tails! Their tails were ornamental, not useful. They couldn't hang by their tails nor did they ever swish them to keep the flies away as horses and cows do. All tiny persons were proud of their tails and tried not to drag them on the floor or in the mud. And, most importantly, they were always careful not to step on one another's tails.

The time finally came when Cousin Dinky was ready to make the first test of Grandpa Little's stove-pump. As Dinky hummed a song off-key, he lit a fire in the heating unit, which was attached to the inside of the basket. It was a quart-sized strawberry basket made of very thin wood. (The basket was the part of the aircraft that hung under the red balloon.)

GRANDPA

DELLA   DINKY

When the fire was hot enough, Dinky opened the hot-air valve. Air was pumped through a tube into the limp balloon, filling it up. Strings from the basket attached to the roof kept the balloon from flying away.

Cousin Dinky saw at once that the hot air was going into the balloon much too fast. He needed to make some adjustments. First he tried to put out the fire by closing off the heat pump. But a nut and bolt were stuck, allowing the hot air to continue flowing into the balloon. The balloon lurched upward as the super-heated air entered it.

"Quick, Tom! Follow me!" yelled Uncle Nick. "We need to get into the basket to add some weight." Tom jumped in after Uncle Nick. "Are the three of us heavy enough to keep the balloon on the roof?" Tom asked.

Just as they got into the basket, Dinky jumped out. "I've got to get my wrench to shut off this stuck valve," he said.

That was a mistake. Without Dinky's weight, the balloon jumped abruptly into the sky, breaking all but one of the holding strings. The balloon tipped and almost everything inside that wasn't fastened down was dumped out.

Tom and Uncle Nick held on tightly to the basket to keep from falling out, too.

When he saw what was happening, Cousin Dinky leaped for the basket. But he couldn't reach it. Dinky ran to the one string that still held down the balloon. Just as he got there — the string broke! Up went the balloon like a shot. Dinky immediately threw the wrench up into the air where it fell into the basket. "This might come in handy!" he called to Uncle Nick.

The balloon rose quickly into the sky. Tom held on to the edge of the basket and looked down. "Uncle Nick!" he yelled. "Everything looks so small. I can't even see Cousin Dinky anymore."

The aircraft was bobbing about and rising fast. The two Littles tried to think what Cousin Dinky had told them about how to fly the balloon. What were they supposed to do with the wrench, anyway? All they could remember was that to make the balloon go higher, they had to throw out some of the pebbles used as ballast. To make it go down, they had to release some of the hot air out of the balloon. They had no control over the direction the balloon went. That depended on which way the wind was blowing.

"Wait a second!" yelled Tom. "I just remembered . . . yeah, I got it!" He looked up and pointed. "Cousin Dinky said there's a valve at the top where the hot air can be let out of the balloon."

Uncle Nick ran to the edge of the basket, hung on to the railing, and leaned out away from the balloon. There was a string dangling right in front of him. He pulled it. The valve on top of the balloon opened. They immediately stopped rising, and began to drop slowly.

After a while Uncle Nick saw the green forest very close beneath them. They were about to crash into the trees! Uncle Nick quickly closed the valve a little, hoping this would give them a bit of lift and keep them going above the treetops.

"That's it!" he yelled, nodding his head and smiling. "We might be able to figure this thing out, Tom."

It was then that Uncle Nick saw the brook beneath them. "Tom!" he yelled, and pointed down. "I think that's the same brook that goes past the Biggs' house. We could follow it back home if we don't get blown off this course."

The balloon continued to fly where the wind pushed it. Uncle Nick and Tom saw a clearing in the woods where a balloon could land. Nick opened and closed the hot-air valve, trying to keep the balloon from rising or falling too fast. Then, a small hill — big to Tinies — rose up in front of them.

In order to keep from crashing into the trees Uncle Nick shut the upper valve all the way so the balloon would rise quickly. Then, suddenly, the balloon got caught in a warm updraft of wind and it shot up the hill in a hurry.

The forest below them was wildly tangled and dark. Tom and Uncle Nick had never seen such a scary, overgrown, wild place. Every now and then Tom had a glimpse of running water through the trees. "Good! We're still following the brook," he said.

Finally, the warm air in the balloon lifted the basket all the way up the side of the hill to the very top.

At that point Tom and Uncle Nick saw a small cleared area studded with sharp rocks below and ahead of them. The brook flowed into and out of a small pond before it began its course down the steep hill into the valley.

The wind hushed for a moment, and the balloon slowed as it approached the landing place. Hoping not to crash into the rocks or the pond, Uncle Nick pulled down all the way on the hot-air valve line to open it completely so the balloon would drop toward the ground quickly. The hot air hissed as it rushed out from the top of the balloon.

The aircraft drifted down toward the clearing in the woods. As they got closer, the ground appeared to rush up to meet them. The Littles, expecting a hard landing, closed their eyes and huddled together. Instead of a bump, the balloon came to a sudden soft stop. The basket tipped over on its side. Tom and Uncle Nick tumbled out into some soft grass. They were on top of a tiny haystack!

As they sat there laughing and hugging each other, a tiny redheaded girl wearing a long, old-fashioned dress came running from between two tall, sharp rocks carrying a pail of yellowish liquid, which she promptly splashed on the side of the haystack beneath them. She looked up at the two Littles. "There's a fire! You two gentlemen should get off that haystack," she said. Then she ran back through the tall rocks with the pail.

Tom and Uncle Nick heard a hissing noise and saw smoke rising from the bottom of the haystack. "There *is* a fire down there!" Tom yelled.

The two Littles slid off the haystack. At this time a tiny boy wearing breeches, a homespun shirt, and a three-cornered hat came running from between the sharp rocks. He was following the tiny girl, who was carrying another pail of the yellowish liquid.

"Glory!" he shouted at the girl. "It not be girl's work to put out dangerous fires! And put your bonnet back on before Father sees you."

THE GIRL, GLORY, paid no attention to the boy. By this time, Tom and Uncle Nick had begun stamping and kicking at the fire as the tiny girl splashed a third pail of the yellow water on the dying embers, which finally put out the fire.

Tom and his uncle saw the fire had been caused by the balloon's hot-air heating stove, which had fallen from the haystack when the balloon crash-landed. The stove lay on the ground. It had a crack in it.

Uncle Nick knelt down and examined the crack in the pump. He looked up and said, "This thing is broken for sure, but not badly. We'll have to find a way to fix it. Nobody should touch it — it's hot! We'll leave it where it is and let it cool off."

The boy came over to them. "Pay my little sister no mind, sirs," he said. "She means well but she often forgets her manners." The boy turned to his sister. "Glory, I won't tell Father what you did if you get back to your chores right away."

The redheaded girl turned quickly and stomped off toward the tall, sharp rocks.

Suddenly, she stopped and looked back at Tom and Uncle Nick. Wiping her hands on her apron, she said, " 'Twas good that you were near 'bout to help when the haystack caught on fire. We could have lost all that hay." Then the tiny girl bowed her head slightly, scowled at her brother, and passed between the tall rocks to enter a nearby barn made of small logs.

"*We* started the fire," Tom told the boy, "by accident."

Uncle Nick nodded. "Tom and I are sorry about that," he said. "We were just trying to land that doggone runaway balloon without getting busted up."

"Pray, what do 'doggone runaway balloon' and 'busted up' mean?" asked the boy.

"Then you didn't see us coming out of the sky in our balloon?" asked Tom.

The boy looked startled. "Mercy," he said, shaking his head. "I know not what you are saying. How could you come from the *sky*?" He stepped back, shaded his eyes with one hand, and looked up at the top of the haystack. The deflated bright red balloon was draped over it, the basket tilted close to the edge. It was kept from falling by the many strings attached to the balloon.

"Pray, who are you?" asked the boy. "From whence did you come? You are not of our village."

"We came from down below," said Uncle Nick. "It's a place called the Big Valley."

Then Tom said, "You know the Big Valley, don't you? It's where all the Tinies live: the House Tinies, Tree Tinies, Brook Tinies, Ground Tinies, and many others." He pointed to Uncle Nick. "My uncle and I are House

Tinies. We live in the walls of Mr. Bigg's house."

"We know nothing of this in our village," said the boy.

"Do you mean you've never seen any other Tinies?" said Tom.

"No," said the boy. "Only the Farm Tinies in our village."

"Uncle Nick," said Tom in a quiet voice, "we must be *really* lost. What is this place?"

"It's amazing," said Uncle Nick. "It means . . . I think . . . that there are tiny people living on top of this hill that have no idea where they are."

"Excuse my disagreeing with you, sirs," said the boy, "but we Farm Tinies know exactly where we are. We're here in our village where we've always been; where our parents and our grandparents and our great-great-grandparents have been for a long, long time — many years, hundreds of years." He scratched his head. "It appears to me, sirs, that you don't know where *you* are!"

Tom looked at Uncle Nick and shrugged his shoulders.

Uncle Nick laughed and said, "Do you know what, Tom? The boy is almost right — *we're* the ones who don't know exactly where we are." He pointed. "However, we are quite sure that this lovely brook winding its way through this place is the same brook that flows right past where we live. Nevertheless, we're quite lost on top of this doggone hill, surrounded by tall, sharp rocks in a tangled, dark, and scary forest without a map!"

Tom rolled his eyes. "Yeah," he said. And in a whisper, "It's *weird*: These people wear strange clothes, talk funny, and don't know what a balloon is."

"Tell us your name, son," said Uncle Nick, "and be kind enough to take us to your parents."

"My name is Justice Nunsuch, sir," said the boy, bowing from the waist. "My sister's name is Miss Glory Nunsuch. Our house is just beyond the sharp rocks."

As TOM AND UNCLE NICK — led by Justice Nunsuch — passed through the sharp rocks, they saw another tiny person coming toward them: a tall, serious-looking man dressed in brown.

"May I introduce my father," said Justice. "Father, these are some tiny people from another place."

The man bowed. "You be strangers," he said. "You came from the *sky*! I saw you."

"Yes, sir, we did," said Uncle Nick. "I am Major Nick Little and this boy with me is my nephew, Tom Little. We landed here accidentally in a balloon. I'm afraid we have caused you and your family some trouble, and we're sorry for that."

"It is not nature's way for men to fly," said the stern-faced Mr. Nunsuch.

Uncle Nick smiled. "You're right about that, sir," he said. "It isn't normal to fly. But the human being can be a stubborn goat. He finds a way to fly anyway." Uncle Nick pointed to the sky. "Haven't you seen those big airplanes pass overhead now and then?"

Mr. Nunsuch looked baffled. "We see birds, that's all. A few of them don't flap their wings, and they make noisy birdcalls — much louder than the other birds. It's a mystery to us; and strange. We've never been able to find their nests as we do with other birds."

Tom said, "Those are airpla —." He stopped and looked up at Uncle Nick, who had grabbed his arm and was shaking his head no.

"Mr. Nunsuch," said Uncle Nick, "we flew up in a balloon by mistake, and we were trying to land the darn thing, but we didn't know how to. We couldn't steer it properly, either, so we landed accidentally on your haystack and — worse luck — started a fire.

"Then — best luck — your daughter, Glory, acted with great speed and had the sense to put out the haystack fire quickly," Uncle Nick went on. "If it weren't for her, sir, our balloon would have been destroyed. This might have made it difficult, if not impossible, for us to return to our home. You've got an amazing girl there!"

Mr. Nunsuch turned quickly to his son. "Justice, if this is so, you have failed to protect your sister," he said in a stern voice. "Putting out fires is *not* women's work!"

"She's fast, Father — I couldn't catch up with her," Justice said. He looked upset.

"That's impossible," said Mr. Nunsuch. "You're a boy and you're bigger and older than she is. I'll talk to you later about your behavior."

"We made a big, dumb mistake," said Uncle Nick, "and we're sorry. As soon as the balloon's pump is repaired, we'll be flying off to our home in the Big Valley. Tell me, Mr. Nunsuch, sir — is there someone hereabouts who can help us fix our hot-air pump? We need it to get the balloon back into the air. I hope you understand we are in a hurry. Our family must be very worried about us."

"Of course!" said Mr. Nunsuch. "Please excuse our bad manners, Major. Justice and I have forgotten our duty to take care of and attend to those in trouble. There is a blacksmith in the village. I will ask him to help you. In the meantime, Justice will take you to our home, where Mrs. Nunsuch will greet you. My dear Major Little, our home is your home until such time as you choose to leave."

Having said that, the man in brown bowed and walked quickly to the log cabin barn. A few moments later he came out mounted on a beautiful, tiny black horse, waved his hand, and galloped off.

Tom and his uncle were astounded. They stood silently watching the man on the horse gallop up a dirt road and disappear over the brow of the hill.

"Wha . . . what's that?" Uncle Nick finally said. "That's not a *horse*. It looks like a horse, but it can't be a horse. There are no tiny horses, and that's a fact."

"It is a horse," whispered Tom, his eyes wide open.

"Justice — what is that animal?" said Uncle Nick. "It looks like a horse, for crying out loud!"

"A horse," said Justice, nodding his head. "Yes, sir, that's what it is."

THE THREE TINY PEOPLE trudged up the hill toward the barn.

Uncle Nick was still stunned at seeing the tiny black horse. "Are there more horses in the barn, Justice?" he asked.

"We have ten horses, yes, sir," answered Justice.

"Wow!" said Tom. *"Ten horses!"*

"What is 'wow,' Tom?" asked Justice.

"It means, ah . . . like, 'gee whiz,' 'cool,' and 'out of sight, man!' " said Tom. "You know — it's great!"

"Tom is very much impressed," said Uncle Nick, "and so am I. We did not know that such a wonder existed in our tiny world."

"Would you like to see the other horses, Tom?" asked Justice.

In the meantime, as this conversation was taking place outside the barn, Glory Nunsuch was inside grooming her favorite among the ten horses owned by the Nunsuch family. She was talking to the animal. "I love you," she whispered, "and one day I'll ride you. I promise."

The horse neighed, nodding its head and flicking its tail, as if agreeing.

Just then the door swung open and Justice, with Uncle Nick and Tom, entered the barn.

"Glory! Are you playing with Lightning again?" asked Justice.

"I'm not *playing* with him, Justice!" said

Glory. "And his name is not Lightning, it's Gentle."

"No, it isn't!"

"Yes, it is!"

Justice turned to the two Littles. "My sister wants to ride, but our parents won't allow her to. She'll get into trouble if they find her on a horse."

"It isn't fair," said Glory. "You get to have a horse and I don't, and I *love* horses!"

"In our village there are twenty-six families. You know the men do men's work and the women do women's work," said Justice. "That's just the way it is, Glory. It's always been that way."

"Riding horses isn't *work*, Justice!" said Glory. "It's fun."

"If Father says you can't ride, then you can't," said Justice.

"But it isn't fair," said Glory. "I can do anything you can do and you know it, Justice Nunsuch."

Justice nodded. "Actually, Glory is faster

than most of the boys in the village," he said.

Glory laughed. "Remember the time I climbed that high rock faster than you did?" she said. "Well, I am *fast*. I don't know why, but my body does things quickly for me. I'll tell you a secret if you don't tell Mother and Father."

"What is it?" said Justice.

"I jumped on a chipmunk's back last week and rode it for a few seconds before I fell off."

"Wow!" said Tom. "That's amazing."

"Glory!" exclaimed Justice. "You shouldn't do that. You're a girl! You might get hurt."

"Do you know how fast chipmunks are? I went twenty-four feet in two seconds," said the smiling tiny girl. "I measured it. That would be two feet if we were big people."

"How'd you know that?" asked Justice.

"I figured it out, Justice," said Glory. "Big people's feet are about twelve inches long and Father's feet are one inch long. It's simple arithmetic."

GLORY SET ABOUT to do her barn chores as Tom and Uncle Nick were taken to the log farmhouse, where they met Mrs. Serenity Nunsuch. She was busy preparing lunch for her family and the visitors from the sky. She never looked up.

Uncle Nick guessed she was low in spirits. "Is there something I can do to help? Set the table, maybe?" he asked.

"Mercy, no," said Mrs. Nunsuch, lowering her head and smiling slightly. "My goodness, Major Little — you're the guests of Mr. Nunsuch. He wouldn't want you to do women's work." She turned to Justice. "Have you seen your sister?" she asked him. "She should be here by now."

"I'll find her," said Tom. He ran out the door and "galloped" down the hill to the barn, pretending he was on Lightning's back.

Glory was standing in the barn's doorway, smiling. "Is it true our brook goes right by your house in the valley?" she asked.

"Uncle Nick thinks so," said Tom. "See those hemlock trees growing along your brook? We have hemlocks, too. They plant themselves near brooks and rivers."

"How did you know that?" Glory asked.

"Grandpa Little told me," said Tom. "He says hemlocks like to keep their toes in the water. I saw a raft in the pond. Do you and Justice paddle around on it?"

Glory laughed. "My brother does, but I'm not supposed to because I'm a girl, so I have to do it when my father is away from home."

"Just think," said Tom, "if that brook wasn't so hard to navigate, you could come and visit us. But, really, you'd probably never get back up the hill. It's too overgrown and awfully steep. Oh, I almost forgot! Your mother wants you. Maybe you should see her before I take a ride on Lightning — er, I mean Gentle."

"It's Gentle," said Glory. "That's what I call him. You should get on Gentle first. Boys get to do everything first in our village because they do everything better, or so my father thinks. Put your foot in the stirrup and swing yourself up into the saddle. You just have to straddle his back."

"I know," said Tom. "I've seen it on TV in the cowboy movies."

"What's that?" said the tiny girl.

"I'll tell you later," said Tom. "It's kind of hard to explain."

Tom stood looking up at the horse.

"Well, don't just stand there, Tom Little," said Glory. "Jump into the saddle!"

"No, thanks," said Tom. "I think I'll climb into it."

"Oh, never mind — I'll show you how to do it!" said Glory. She ran toward the horse. Tom tackled her. "No, you won't — I'll do it!" he yelled as they fell together in the hay, laughing.

Glory struggled to get loose from Tom. He shoved her deeper into the straw pile and ran toward the horse, scrambling to mount the animal. The tiny boy got one foot in a stirrup and was kicking with the other foot, trying to swing into the saddle, when Gentle decided to gallop through the door into the barnyard.

Quick as a flash, Glory ran to the next stall and jumped from the ground right onto the horse's bare back.

Using the heels of her feet, she directed the horse swiftly out the door. Around and around went the two horses in the barnyard. Finally, Gentle jumped the fence and galloped up the road toward the house, with Tom Little draped across the saddle on his stomach, hanging on desperately.

Glory came racing up from behind. As she got close to Tom and Gentle she hopped to her feet on the horse's broad back, holding her arms out for balance.

The tiny girl jumped. She landed right on top of Tom Little. "Whumpth!" he cried out. "Oh, that hurt! Thanks."

Glory pulled the reins and Gentle came to a stop. The other horse ran back toward the barn. "Are you all right?" Glory asked Tom, who had managed to sit up behind her in the saddle.

"I guess so," he said. "That was some ride."

In a few minutes, Glory had both horses safely in their stalls.

As Glory and Tom walked out of the barn, Mr. Nunsuch returned from the village. "Glory," he said, "don't you have chores to do?"

"I finished them, Father," said Glory.

The lunch bell rang. Glory ran off toward the house.

"Mr. Nunsuch, sir," said Tom. "Your daughter is an amazing person. She is —"

Mr. Nunsuch interrupted Tom. "Mrs. Nunsuch and I pray that she will be a *dutiful* girl whom we can be proud of. When she is a woman she will need to be — first of all — a steady helpmate to her husband."

Tom thought to himself: Glory probably saved me from getting badly hurt, and I can't even tell her father about it because she was riding a horse, which girls aren't supposed to do in this place. Boy! Am I glad I don't live here!

UNCLE NICK AND TOM were having lunch with the Nunsuches. Glory had set the table and was serving the food. She gave Tom a wink and a smile every time she passed him. Tom was trying to keep from laughing.

Uncle Nick said to Mr. Nunsuch, "I'm pleased that the blacksmith can repair our hot-air stove-pump. I believe that the balloon maker, our cousin Dinky, might be searching for us. With luck Tom and I may be out of your way today or tomorrow."

"Ohhh!" said Glory, looking at her parents. "Can't the Littles stay for a little while longer? They're not in our way, are they, Mother and Father?"

"Glory, remember your manners, child," said Mr. Nunsuch.

"Please, Glory," said Mrs. Nunsuch in a quiet, calm voice, her head down. "You must try not to speak at table unless you are spoken to. You are a child, after all."

When everyone finished eating, there was a long silence in the room. Finally Uncle Nick said, "Mr. Nunsuch, since we will probably not be here much longer, I would be very interested in learning about the tiny people in your village; how they got here, where they came from — your history, in fact, sir."

"It's a simple story and I'd be pleased to relate it to you and the boy," said Mr. Nunsuch. He turned to Glory. "You may get up from the table now, Glory, and help your mother with the dishwashing and cleanup."

Glory's face fell. "Oh, but Father, I would love it so if I could hear the story."

Mr. Nunsuch didn't say a word. He pointed to the door.

Glory bowed to everyone and walked slowly from the room. "Oh, well," she said to herself. "I know most of the story anyway, and Justice will tell me if there's anything new."

"It's a simple story," said Mr. Nunsuch again. "The tiny people in our village are descendants of some of the tiny Pilgrims who came to America by boat and landed at Plymouth Rock in 1620."

"Father," Justice said, "tell them about how they got off the boat — that's fun." He laughed.

Mr. Nunsuch looked crossly at his son. "Justice, I'm about to tell the whole story. You must learn to be patient, son — it's a virtue."

Justice looked glum. "I'm sorry, sir. It won't happen again."

Mr. Nunsuch continued his story: "Of course, the big people on the boat had no idea that our forefathers were on the boat with them. The Tinies were the last to get off by climbing down the anchor chains and

ropes along with the rats that deserted the ship when they saw land after a long and difficult voyage."

He paused and looked at Justice. "And it wasn't exactly *fun*, Justice — probably it was somewhat frightening, actually.

"It was a hard life for them at first," Mr. Nunsuch continued, "but as the big Pilgrims built houses and farms there were places for the Tinies to live secretly in the walls and ceilings of the buildings. There weren't many tiny people and the small amounts of food they took from the big people were hardly noticed.

"Then came the time of wars between the big people. Our tiny great-great-great-grandfathers were never sure how the wars started and whose fault it was, but every time there was a battle, it seemed to happen right in front of them!

"Houses were destroyed and some of our ancestors were killed. Each time there was a war, our tiny people packed up everything on their horses and goats and hurried off down the road looking for a peaceful place to start over again."

"Goats!" exclaimed Tom Little, paying no attention to Mr. Nunsuch's need for silence when he speaks. "You have tiny goats as well as horses?"

"It must have been yellow goat's milk that Glory threw on the fire, Tom," said Uncle Nick.

"To go on with this historical account," said the farmer impatiently, "our ancestors wandered across the land looking for a peaceful place away from wars. They fled from wars in towns like Concord, Yorktown, and other places, always heading westward trying to get away from war."

"Well," said Uncle Nick, "you certainly ended up at a quiet and peaceful place. I've been told by tiny explorers from the Big Valley that they couldn't get up this hill you're living on. The very dense underbrush and steep terrain kept them away."

"The forefathers made our village so difficult to get to that even we who live here cannot find our way out," said Mr. Nunsuch. He added, "Not that we want to. We like our isolation. No big people ever come here."

"What about the brook that comes through the place?" said Tom.

"A few of our folks tried sailing down the stream on rafts," said Mr. Nunsuch. "They never came back. That was the end of that."

"Then you'll have to stay!" said Justice to Tom. "What fun we'll have!"

"Justice!" said Mr. Nunsuch. "This is a serious problem for the Littles, not a happy thing."

"I don't think there will be a problem, sir," said Uncle Nick. "Our cousin Dinky, the family's adventurer, has survived many such difficulties, and I'm sure he will be able to get us out of here."

"Oh, yes," said Mr. Nunsuch, "that's the gentleman who, ahem, flies in the air like a bird. Well, I hope you are right, but I see great problems with getting back to your home that way." Then in a loud whisper to himself: "Flying, indeed!"

Uncle Nick smiled. "You will see for yourself, sir, and soon. Be prepared for a big surprise. Living on the top of this hill away from other tiny folks has kept your community from learning of the many changes that have taken place since 1776."

"Well, that may be so, Major Little, but I can assure you that we have a way of life very much like that our forefathers enjoyed, and except for our terrible war experiences, we wouldn't change it for all the tea in the Boston Tea Party."

Uncle Nick laughed and said, "I like a person who sticks up for where he lives and the people he knows." He cleared his throat. "Ahem! However, *everything* in a way of life isn't always right," Uncle Nick said. "For instance, there were big people who were slaves back in the old days. That wasn't right and in 1865, President Abraham Lincoln put an end to that during the Civil War."

"I didn't know that!" said Farmer Nunsuch. "That's wonderful! Forcing folks into slavery is a terrible thing."

Uncle Nick said, "There were many other changes that took place as the years went by — one of them may surprise you and Mrs. Nunsuch, and you may not like it."

"Pray, go ahead with your interesting information, Major," said Mr. Nunsuch. "You've caught my interest. What is it?"

Major Little took a deep breath, then said quickly, "Most big and tiny people in the United States of America today believe that women are equal to men and girls are equal to boys and they should be treated the same."

"What is this United States of America? What have these people done to our country?!" said Mr. Nunsuch. "I . . . I . . ." he stammered. "Justice, you may leave the table. This talk is not for your ears."

Quick as a wink, Tom and Justice were through the door and out of the house.

Mrs. Nunsuch and Glory were working outside. "Justice!" Mrs. Nunsuch said, handing him an acorn shell on a string. "I'm going

to make honey cakes for dinner this evening, and there is no honey in the pantry. Fetch some from the beehive while those two men inside the house decide how to solve the problems of the world." She grinned shyly and went back into the house.

Justice tossed the acorn to Glory. "I just remembered!" he said. "Father told me to groom a horse for Major Little to ride with him into town, and I forgot. Could you do me a small favor and fetch the honey for Mother while I'm getting the horse ready — it's easy."

He started running toward the barn.

"Why, of course, my dear brother!" Glory shouted. "Only it's not a small favor and it isn't easy — so you owe me *two* favors."

Justice stopped and turned around in his tracks, laughing. "Glory!" he yelled. "You may be my equal, but please don't think you are *better* than I am! That would be a big mistake." He laughed all the way to the barn.

"Let's go to the beehive, Tom," said Glory. She began to run. Tom was right behind her.

"Do you want to race to the place?" asked Glory, still in front.

"How can I do that?" said Tom. "If I get ahead of you, I won't know where I'm going."

"It's in that old apple tree in the hollow on the edge of the woods," said Glory, pointing.

"Hey!" yelled Tom. He touched Glory's shoulder and pointed to the right. "What's that over there?"

Glory hesitated and looked to the right as Tom sped past her on the left. He was well ahead by the time she realized that he had tricked her.

They were both laughing when Tom got to the apple tree first.

"You cheated!" said Glory, giving him a push.

"I know," said Tom. "I'm sorry. I went bananas."

"Bananas? What do you mean?" Glory said.

Tom thought, then said, "Going bananas means going nuts, or crazy . . . off the wall. Do you know what I mean?"

"No."

"Okay, I'll have to figure it out later so you can understand it. Where's the honey?"

Glory pointed to a hole in the decayed trunk of the tree. "That's the place," she said. "Do you see those bees going in and out?"

"Yep," said Tom.

"We have to shoo them away and climb into their hive and take some honey," said Glory, holding up the acorn basket.

"Oh," said Tom, "I get it. We have to commit suicide trying to take some honey away from the bees so your mother can make honey cakes."

Just then they heard a crashing noise. "It's a bear coming through the woods," Glory whispered fiercely. "Look at the treetops, they're swinging back and forth. He's coming to get some honey, too, and he's bumping into the trees, crashing through the forest. That's what bears do when there isn't enough room — they make their own way!"

"Holy cow!" said Tom. "What'll we do?"

"Hide!" said Glory. She and Tom ran to a nearby bush behind the apple tree and dove into a small hole in the ground.

"It's a chipmunk hole — I come here all the time," explained Glory. "I've got some of the 'chips' trained. Take a peek outside, Tom — the bear is a magnificent beast."

The two Tinies stuck their heads out of the hole. The bear was ambling up to the honey tree. The ground shook.

"Wow!" whispered Tom. "He's as big as Godzilla! And do you know what? He smells awful! What a stink!!"

The huge animal stood up on his hind legs and reached into the hole where the honey was. Using his big paw, he pulled out a chunk of the dripping honeycomb. He shoved it into his mouth while his second paw went down into the honeycomb.

Hundreds of bees took to the air and began attacking the bear to drive him away. He kept right on eating.

"Now we get *our* honey," whispered Glory.

She popped up out of the chipmunk hole with Tom right behind her. They began climbing the back side of the tree, going up twig by twig.

The bear decided he had had enough and began his retreat. The angry bees attacked him again and again. As the satisfied bear lumbered away from the tree licking his paws, the two tiny kids got to the honeycomb. They quickly filled the acorn shell with honey. Glory looped the string over her shoulder and covered the honey with the acorn cap.

"We're outta here!" yelled Tom.

"No, we're not, Tom," said Glory. "We still have to climb down the tree and get away from here before the bees come back."

"Yeah, that's what I meant," said Tom.

"But it's not what you said," insisted Glory. "My goodness, you folks from the Big Valley sure talk funny."

WHEN THEY ARRIVED back at the
Nunsuches' house, Tom and Glory discov-
ered Cousin Dinky dangling from a tall bush
in the front yard. His parachute suspension
lines were caught in the branches. He was
slowly swinging to and fro, shaking his head,
a wide smile on his face. In a few moments
he cut himself loose and came down from
the bush.

"This is the amazing Glory," said Tom to
Cousin Dinky. "She's my new friend."

"Hi, Glory," said Cousin Dinky. "Where
am I?"

"You are on our farm in our front yard,"
said Glory. "How did you get here?"

"I followed the brook," Cousin Dinky said.
"I always follow brooks. Lost people usually
follow a brook because it will lead them *out*

of the woods. This time I decided Nick and Tom had probably been blown up the hill to the top."

Cousin Dinky pointed to the sky and waved. "There goes Della!" he said. "She's heading for home in her glider."

"Della's his wife," Tom explained to Glory. "She was flying the glider that Dinky jumped from. He's going to repair our balloon so we can fly home."

"Do you mean there's a woman flying in that thing, making it go?" said Glory. "How could that be?"

"Della's a good pilot," Tom said. "She knows what she's doing."

"But she's a woman," said Glory. "Women can't fly, can they?"

Cousin Dinky said, "They can if they learn how to, Glory."

"Oh! That's wonderful!" said Glory. She ran into the house to tell her mother.

Justice came walking up the path from the barn to see what was going on. He looked at the parachute in the bush and Cousin Dinky on the ground. Then he looked at Tom. "I missed something important, didn't I?" he said.

Tom nodded. "Cousin Dinky jumped out of the glider, fell toward the ground, pulled the rip cord to open the parachute, and landed in this bush," said Tom. "We missed seeing all of it."

Justice laughed. "So if no one saw it, there is no proof," he said. "Hah! It's a mystery."

Just then Uncle Nick and Mr. Nunsuch came into the yard on horseback, returning from their ride. "It's not a mystery, Justice," said Mr. Nunsuch. "The major and I saw the glider and the parachute jump and the landing. It's really true! People can fly in the air. I can't get over it. It's . . . magnificent."

Cousin Dinky's eyes looked like saucers. He stammered, "What, er . . ." He pointed. "Those are *tiny* horses!" He turned to Uncle Nick. "Did I land on my head? Am I in cuckoo land? There are no tiny horses, right?" He pinched himself hard. "OUCH!" he said. "I'm not asleep. It must be true."

"We have goats, too," said Justice. "All the other farm animals died out years ago."

Just then, Glory came out the front door with her mother, who, smiling happily for once, was cradling something furry and white. Glory held a tiny bit of black fur.

"Cats!" said Tom. "You have tiny cats, too? I didn't see them in the house."

"They are shy at first with strangers," Mrs. Nunsuch said.

Glory handed her black cat to the amazed Tom. "Incredible!" he said as he stroked the soft fur. The cat purred and licked his hand.

"Our forefathers believed that cats were good luck," Glory told him, "so they kept their cats very safe and comfortable on the trail west. Ever since, we have had cats on our farm."

Glory's mother added, "This beautiful white-haired cat, Rosie, is fourteen years old. Glory's black cat, called Squeaky, is the great-great-great-grandson of Rosie and would rather squeak than say meow!"

After admiring the cats, Cousin Dinky and Mr. Nunsuch took the cracked hot-air pump to the village, where under Cousin Dinky's directions the blacksmith repaired it.

They brought the pump back to the Nunsuch farm and went right to work attaching it to the red balloon's basket.

"What luck!" Cousin Dinky said. "The

wrench I threw into the basket when the balloon broke away is still here. I can sure use this thing to loosen that stuck valve." As Cousin Dinky and Uncle Nick worked at the task, the tiny pilot explained what he was doing and how the stove-pump worked. The Nunsuch family was fascinated. In a short time the work was done.

Cousin Dinky turned to the family and bowed low. "That's it, folks," he said. They clapped their hands in admiration.

"Excellent!" said Mr. Nunsuch.

Justice grinned at his dad.

Cousin Dinky looked up at the clouds moving across the sky. "The wind is blowing in the right direction to fly the balloon home," he said. He turned to Tom and Uncle Nick. "The family is very worried about the two of you. We need to leave now."

"Oh, no!" said Glory. She ran to Tom. "It's too soon. We've just begun to be friends. You can't go . . . so soon." Tears welled up in her eyes.

"Glory!" said Mr. Nunsuch. "Behave yourself! You're acting like, like . . . a girl!"

Mrs. Nunsuch put her arms around Glory. "For heaven's sake, Mr. Nunsuch, she *is* a girl!"

Tom looked at Cousin Dinky. "Could I . . . could we write letters to each other?" he said. "I could tell her all about our adventures and Glory could tell me about theirs."

"We could try, Tom," said Cousin Dinky. "When the wind is right I could fly up here and parachute letters to Glory and the Nunsuches. But I need to figure out how I can pick up their mail from here." He looked at Mr. Nunsuch.

"I'm not so sure that we should do this," said Mr. Nunsuch. "We Farm Tinies have kept to ourselves for many years and we have our own ways of doing things. I think that we might have trouble if our ways are changed by too much contact between our families."

"No, Father, no!" yelled Glory. She burst into tears.

"It's too late, Mr. Nunsuch," said his wife. "Glory already knows there are places where women and girls are treated as equal to men and boys."

"Well, my dear Mrs. Nunsuch," said Mr. Nunsuch, "we don't need ideas like that in this place, and as long as I am the husband and father here, we won't have them!"

Uncle Nick spoke softly to Cousin Dinky. "It's time to go, Dinky." He turned to Mr. Nunsuch. "Mr. Nunsuch, sir, we appreciate what you have done for us. You have a great way of life here and we honor and respect it. We certainly hope we have not disturbed you too much with our foreign actions or opinions. It's a big world and there's room for many different ways of living and understanding what life is all about.

"We hope you will remember us fondly, as we will remember you. It has been a most interesting time in our lives."

Suddenly, a large number of Farm Tinies from the village arrived at the scene. They

wanted to meet the strangers from the Big
Valley who flew in the sky in a magical flying
machine.

Uncle Nick, Tom, and Cousin Dinky
shook hands with all the people.

Then Uncle Nick climbed into the balloon's basket. "All aboard, Littles!" he yelled.

Cousin Dinky fired up the hot-air pump,
opened a valve, and the aircraft began to rise.

Tom hung over the edge of the basket, waving at the Nunsuches.

Glory broke away from her mother's embrace and ran toward Tom. At the last moment she made a great leap up and touched his reaching hand. "Don't ever forget me, Tom!" she cried out.

"I won't," Tom said. "I'll come back someday."

"Honest?"

"Honest."

In a few moments the balloon was a red dot in the sky, heading down off the steep hill.

A MONTH LATER, Tom Little and his younger sister, Lucy, were in the living room of the Littles' apartment in the walls of Mr. Bigg's house.

Tom was retelling his and Uncle Nick's adventures among the Farm Tinies — and especially those exciting moments with Glory Nunsuch. Tom had gotten along very well with Glory. He liked and admired her.

"The trouble is, Lucy," Tom said, "I didn't get to know her as much as I wanted to. I felt so sorry for her because she was actually living in the old days — the very old days — back in the eighteenth century, probably, up on top of that hill."

Tom stopped talking and began to shake his head. "Her father wouldn't even allow her to write to me!" he said.

"It's too bad," said Lucy. "I wish she could write to us."

"Well, anyway," said Tom. "Let's talk about this book I'm reading, *The Adventures of Tom Sawyer*."

Tom was very excited about the book. He had "borrowed" it from Mr. Bigg's son, Henry. Lucy had helped him carry the paperback book to the Littles' apartment.

Lucy had read the book some time ago. She said, "It's a boys' book. Girls don't get a chance to be heroes in the story like boys do."

"Sure they do!" said Tom. "Becky Thatcher is lost in the dark cave along with Tom Sawyer."

"When Becky and Tom are lost in the cave," said Lucy, "Becky is the scared one who sits down holding the string so Tom Sawyer can walk around looking for a way out of the cave. What kind of a hero is Becky, sitting there, scared? Can't she do the exploring sometimes?"

"Well, sure," said Tom, "but mostly boys are better at that kind of thing than girls, don't you think?"

"Well," said Lucy, "Daddy says I have a good sense of direction. Remember that time when you —"

"All right, all right," said Tom, waving his hand.

"And what about that girl Glory?" said Lucy. "It seems to me she could be ten times braver than Tom Sawyer, and she's real — not in a book!"

"I know," said Tom. "She's amazing. She can do anything. I wish she were here sometimes, you know."

"Maybe you'll see her again," said Lucy quietly.

"Anyway," said Tom, "what I want to do is find a tiny cave with a secret back entrance like the one Tom Sawyer found. I think it would be fun to hang out there."

"Well, *I* want to find a place for a secret garden, just like the one Mary Lennox found in the book called *The Secret Garden*," said Lucy.

"Hey, yeah — that's cool," said Tom Little. "I like that book a lot, too."

Suddenly, Tom jumped up. "I've got an idea, Lucy," he said.

"I hope it's not going to be something you want me to do to help you find a cave," said Lucy.

"Just listen, Lucy. You might change your mind. Why don't we find my cave first and make your secret garden right next to it?" suggested Tom. "Then we can help each other."

Lucy thought for a moment. Then she said, "Tom — cross your heart and hope to die if you don't help me with the secret garden after we find your cave. Okay?"

"You don't trust me?" asked Tom. "Glory Nunsuch would have helped me just like this." He snapped his fingers.

"We used to be afraid of the dark when we were small kids, Tom," Lucy said. "Is that why you want me to help you, because caves are dark?"

"I'm not afraid," Tom scoffed. "*You* see better in the dark than I do, that's all."

"You must cross your heart, Tom," said Lucy. "Remember?"

The tiny boy crossed his heart with his forefinger and solemnly spoke: "I hope to get real sick if I don't help you after we find my cave," he said.

"Hey! That's not right," said Lucy. She laughed. "You're supposed to *die* if you don't help me make the secret garden."

"I changed my mind," Tom said. "I'm not dying — no way!"

"I didn't say you had to die," said Lucy, laughing. "I said you had to 'hope' to die."

"Good!" said Tom. "Let's get started!"

"Where are we going to look for your cave?" said Lucy.

"I've got an idea," said Tom. "The best way to get into the woods is to hitchhike a ride with Henry Bigg and his friends when they go to their hideout. There are probably some tiny caves around there."

The next day, Tom and Lucy sneaked aboard a crate that Henry and his friends had loaded with snack foods, soft drinks, blankets, and tools for making their hideout.

As the boys trudged on, Tom and Lucy peeked out through the slats in the crate.

"Tom," said Lucy, "we're going far away from home. Is it all right?"

"We're okay," said Tom. "We'll get back. I'm memorizing the route."

"So am I!" said Lucy.

They both laughed.

Finally, Henry and his friends stopped in a small clearing in the woods.

After making sure there were no "enemies" lurking about and spying on them, the boys pushed their way through some thickly tangled vines and leaves and entered their camouflaged hideout.

The tiny children climbed out of the crate and made their way to the other side of the clearing, a good distance away from Henry Bigg and his friends.

They heard water gurgling. "We're near the brook that goes by Glory's village and the Biggs' house," said Tom. "This may be a good place to look for the cave."

The two Littles searched the area. Before long, Lucy spotted a small hole in the ground next to a log.

"Here's one! I'm first to find it!" she yelled, and promptly fell to her hands and knees and entered the hole. In a few moments she came out. "It's pitch-black," she announced.

"We'll have a light in there in a jiffy," said Tom. "Here, hold one of these birthday candles while I light it."

Holding her lit candle, Lucy led the way into the cave through the small hole. Once inside, the tiny children found that the cave or tunnel was large enough for them to stand up.

Lucy was carrying a small bobbin — a spool of thread — she had borrowed from Mrs. Bigg's sewing room. The tiny children thought they might need it in case they got lost in the cave and had to find a way out without getting mixed up — just as Tom Sawyer and Becky Thatcher did, using a ball of string for the same purpose.

The first thing the children noticed in the cave was the many small rooms or chambers. In one room were stored thousands of tree seeds and nuts. In another, leaves, berries, buds, mushrooms, fruit — even dead insects like cicadas and grasshoppers. Another chamber was a toilet.

"Tom," said Lucy, "an animal lives here."

"I know. It's cool," said Tom. "It's almost like that place where the treasure was when Tom Sawyer and Huck Finn found it, only this is like the animal's treasure, right?"

"Won't they be mad at us for sneaking around their property?" said Lucy. "What if they're mice? I'm afraid of them."

"We won't touch their stuff," said Tom. "And remember, we have the candle. Animals are afraid of fire. If we meet any scary animals, they'll hightail it out of here. C'mon — this is exciting! Let's explore!"

Soon the tiny children were in a tunnel that was going deeper into the earth. They passed more tunnels that branched off in other directions. Tom was looking for a secret back door. "It's got to be here someplace," he said.

"How do you know there is one?" asked Lucy.

"Most animals have back exits to escape if they need to. This is probably a chipmunk cave and chipmunks have lots of back exits."

They came to a large room — much larger than the others — with a ten-inch-high ceiling. The candle flickered and went out. It was pitch-black in the room.

"Tom! What'll we do?" said Lucy.

"Here," said Tom, "hold out your hand and take this candle. I'm getting another match."

Tom felt around in the dark for a stone and struck the match on the stone. The match fizzled for a few seconds, smoking furiously, then died. It was dark again, and Tom and Lucy choked on the smoke.

They stood silently, holding their breaths. There! The smoke was gone.

"Phew!!" said Tom. Lucy coughed.

"This means," said Tom, "we have one

more match, so we have to start back now. If it fizzles and we can't light the candle, we'll be in the dark like this when we try to find our way out."

"What will we do?" said Lucy.

"Start hoping it'll be okay," said Tom, "and cross our fingers. But first, let's set up the spool so we can unroll the thread as we go along. That way we can find our way back to-morrow if we want to keep on exploring."

"You should have thought of doing that string thing when we started coming in here," said Lucy.

"I made a mistake, Lucy!" said Tom. "Give me a break, will you?"

Tom laid the bobbin of thread on the ground. The tiny boy worked slowly, feeling with his hands because of the darkness of the cave. He took a small nail from his backpack, put it into the hole in the center of the spool, and hammered it into the dirt floor with a rock. Then, when he pulled on the thread, the spool spun around.

When there was enough thread off the spool, Tom tied it around his waist.

"Okay, Lucy," he said. "I'm going to light the last match. Cross your fingers, arms, and legs — and hope it works."

"Tom, that's silly."

"I know," said Tom, "but it can't hurt and it might help, as Grandpa says. Maybe it'll help a little: Here goes!"

The tiny boy struck the last match on a stone. It flared immediately into a bright flame. He then lit the candle.

Lucy blinked in the bright light and saw something run from the chamber. "I saw an animal," she whispered.

"What kind of animal?" said Tom.

"I don't know. I only saw its tail."

"Maybe it's a *tiny person*, Lucy!"

"The tail was bushier than our tails . . . I think," said Lucy.

Just then, from the opposite direction, the children heard a soft *chuck, chuck, chuck* sound — so fast that it almost became a songlike trill that a bird might use to warn people away from them.

"I think it's a chipmunk!" Tom said. "I saw its tail, too, but I can't be sure."

The two Littles walked back up the tunnel, retracing their steps. Every now and then the chipmunk (or whatever it was) almost showed itself and then immediately disappeared.

"Lucy," whispered Tom, "it's acting like it's trying to lead us safely out of the cave."

"Yeah," said Lucy. "Maybe."

"I wish Glory were here," said Tom. "She knows a lot about animals, especially chip-munks."

Eventually they came to the cave entrance, and the animal had vanished. Tom untied the thread around his waist and tied it to a root.

Outside the cave, Tom said, "That animal *was* leading us out of the place . . . I think."

"I know, I know," said Lucy. "It was like something a dog would do."

"Like a story in a book," Tom added. "Lassie or something. Let's get back to Henry Bigg's hideout so we can hitch a ride back home in the crate."

Along the way, Lucy saw a bright flash coming from somewhere under a nearby bush. It turned out to be a large, widemouthed glass bottle lying on its side in the leaves and twigs, reflecting the sun into their eyes.

"There's some dirt in the bottle, Tom," said Lucy, "and something is *growing* in there!"

Sure enough, grass was growing inside the bottle. And, halfway up one of the grass blades was a tiny flower.

Lucy stooped over and climbed into the bottle through its wide neck. "It's a beautiful blue-eyed grass flower," she said. "Tom, I've found my secret garden."

AT DINNER THAT NIGHT, Tom and Lucy told everyone about their adventure in the woods.

". . . and when we were trying to get out of the cave because our matches were used up," said Tom, "an *animal* of some kind, maybe a chipmunk — we couldn't tell for sure — acted like it was leading us out."

"Yeah," said Lucy, nodding her head. "It was spooky."

"Well," said Mr. Little, "what I'm concerned about is that you went too far from the house without an adult with you."

"We didn't know that Henry and his friends would go that far away, Dad," said Tom. "We won't go there again."

Lucy stamped her foot.

"Darn it!" she said. "I found that perfect secret garden for nothing. I was figuring out how to plant more tiny flowers in that bottle by the cave. Now we can't go back there because it's too far away!"

"Hold it there, kids," said Uncle Nick. "Don't bust your britches or break your hearts. If it's okay with your parents, I'll go along with the two of you next time. We can look into this mystery of a chipmunk guide after we transplant your flowers into the secret garden bottle."

Uncle Nick turned to Mr. Little. "I think the kids have come up with a jim-dandy adventure." He winked at Tom and Lucy.

Uncle Nick had a way of settling things, so it was settled.

A few days later Henry Bigg and his friends transported the usual supplies to their hideout in the crate — along with Tom, Lucy, and Uncle Nick.

The sun was shining when the Littles got to Lucy's bottle. Sunbeams came through the forest roof and were shining directly into the glass.

"Isn't that lucky!" Lucy said. "The sunbeams will help my flowers grow like magic."

The flowers Lucy brought were all tiny ones that she had dug up, roots and all, from the Biggs' lawn. Being tiny, they had been so close to the ground that Mr. Bigg's lawn mower hadn't cut them down.

"These flowers are just the right size for tiny people," said Lucy. "I wonder if big people ever look closely at tiny flowers and see that they look just as well-made and beautiful as big flowers."

"Right you are, Lucy," said Uncle Nick. "It just goes to show you that Mother Nature takes as much care in creating her tiny masterpieces as she does with her big ones."

"It's the same thing with a big horse and the tiny horses that Glory and I rode at the Nunsuch farm," said Tom. "The only difference between them is size."

"I always thought that tiny flowers were made for tiny people," said Lucy. "That's what Granny Little says."

"But if they were made for tiny people," said Tom, "why aren't there other tiny things like tiny apple trees with tiny apples, things like that?"

"Tom, don't forget about the tiny cats, horses, and goats at Glory's village!" said Lucy.

"Here's what I think," said Uncle Nick. "All of us tiny people living in America are descended from the tiny people who landed at Plymouth Rock in 1620 and maybe from Tinies who landed in Jamestown in 1619. All the rest of the Tinies live in other countries, always have. That's where all the tiny trees, animals, flowers, birds, fish — the whole kit and caboodle — are, except for the few creatures, plants and so forth, that were brought to our country by tiny people like the Nunsuches' ancestors."

The Littles had gotten busy planting flowers in the glass bottle while they were talking. After a while, Lucy went up and down the rows of flowers pointing to them. "There are the wood violets, the true forget-me-nots, the common strawberry, ground ivy, Indian pipe, common wood sorrel, and the rue anemone."

"Lucy! You know all their names!" said Tom in admiration.

"I looked them all up in Mr. Bigg's flower book," said Lucy, "and memorized them."

"Oh! For a moment I thought you were a genius," Tom said.

"I probably *am* a genius, Tom," said his sister with a sly smile. "Now, where's the water for the flowers?"

"Don't remind me of the brook," said Tom. "It's the same brook that goes right by Glory's . . . er, I mean the Nunsuch farm, where all those tiny horses are. I wish I were riding on one right now!" He paused, thinking. Then he said, "Mr. Nunsuch doesn't know anything about kids." He stamped off to fetch water from the brook.

When they finished planting and watering the tiny flowers, Uncle Nick picked up his bow and arrow.

"Now," he said, "let's try to get to the bottom of this business of a mysterious animal that appears and disappears and seemed to lead you out of the cave."

"It gives me goose bumps," Lucy said.

"We need to know what's going on," Uncle

Nick continued. "We can't have you two kids wandering around in a cave that strange or dangerous animals are living in. Chipmunks are probably okay, shrews are not."

Tom lit the candle Uncle Nick was holding and they all entered the cave.

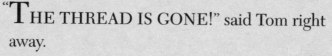

"THE THREAD IS GONE!" said Tom right away.

Uncle Nick said, "We'll just have to find our way without the thread."

"We came from that direction," Tom pointed. "I think."

Shortly after starting out, the Littles came to a chamber with a drowsy mother chipmunk nursing her babies.

"There *are* chipmunks in the cave!" whispered Lucy.

Uncle Nick put his finger to his lips. "Shhh!" he said. "Walk on by quietly."

"I don't remember that place," Tom said.

"Here, Tom," said his uncle. "Hold the candle while I string an arrow in my bow just in case we need it."

"Please don't kill any animals, Uncle Nick," Lucy said.

Uncle Nick, who had been a soldier for most of his life and knew how to handle weapons properly, said, "Don't worry, Lucy, I would only give them a warning shot in case there are any nasties in here."

They went on. In the light from the candle, they could see that the dirt tunnel was changing. The ceiling looked like it was covered with wood. A little farther along the bottom and sides seemed to be all wood, too.

"This is *not* where Lucy and I were," said Tom.

Lucy nodded her head.

"We must be inside the tree roots!" said Uncle Nick.

"We're going into the tree," Tom guessed.

"This is weird," announced Lucy.

"Right!" said Tom. "Terrific!"

Then the tunnel began to rise. Everyone, especially Uncle Nick, had to duck down a bit to climb up what they guessed was the inside of the tree trunk.

"Haven't we gone far enough?" asked Lucy.

"We'll turn around soon," Uncle Nick said.

Suddenly, they heard a scolding, chattering voice. They all turned toward the noise just in time to see a small animal streak past them at terrific speed.

"It's got to be a chipmunk!" said Tom. "Glory says they can go twenty-four tiny feet in two seconds. She figured it out. They become almost invisible — blurred — from where they start to run to where they stop."

Then the Littles heard someone walking toward them. A figure came slowly out of the darkness. "Tom," she said. "It's me, Glory."

"Glory!!" yelled Tom. "Is it really you? What are you doing here?"

Uncle Nick walked quickly to the tiny girl and hugged her. Everyone talked at the same time.

Glory said, "I got lost in the brook on the raft days and days ago. I'm so glad you found me." She began to tremble. Tears came into her eyes.

"Glory!" yelled Tom. "You came down that brook this far on a *raft*? That's crazy! Why'd you do that? Did you run away from home?"

Glory shook her head no.

"Take it easy, Tom," said Uncle Nick, his arm around the tiny girl.

Lucy reached out and touched Glory. "I'm Tom's sister, Lucy," she said. "Tom says you're amazing. Did you tame that chipmunk?"

Glory nodded.

". . . and you ride on it?"

"Yes, sometimes. He's my friend."

"Glory," said Uncle Nick quietly, "what happened with the raft?"

Glory took a deep breath and began her story:

"Sometimes I paddle around the pond, at night, so my father won't see me," she said. "I've done that a lot.

"One night a little rain fell and I began to paddle for the shore," she went on. "Suddenly there was no more moon. Just like that — it was dark and very windy. The wind and the rain fell on me and knocked me over.

I grabbed the rope handle that was on the raft and held on tight. Then the water in the pond swelled up. The waves pushed the raft toward the dam. It was hard to see, but I felt myself going up and over the dam, and into the brook. I was trying to hold on, and that's all I can remember."

"That was probably a flash flood," said Uncle Nick. "We had one in the valley last month. I'll bet it was the same one. So the way I figure it, you've been away from home for a month."

Glory nodded and continued. "When I woke up, it was still dark and raining but not so hard. I must have tied the rope around myself, but I didn't remember doing it. The raft had gotten stuck on some vines. I swung from one of them to the ground and looked for a place out of the rain."

"And you found this chipmunk hole," suggested Tom.

"Right," said Glory. "I crawled in the dark into the hole until I smelled their scent and found one of their rooms. They were all asleep together, the mother and father and four chipmunk babies. The babies were just beginning to grow hair. I snuggled up against the mother and father and when he began to make noises, I made a few back to him that calmed him down."

"Holy cow, Glory!" said Tom. "Did that really happen?"

"Surely it did, Tom," replied Glory. "You didn't think I was going to sleep in the rain, did you?"

11

BACK IN THE Littles' apartment that evening, the tiny family learned about Glory's accidental raft trip down the brook and her stay with the chipmunks.

Grandpa Little said, "You lived for a time with the chipmunks. What was that like?"

Glory nodded. "It wasn't easy, but I knew something about them from taming some of them at home — a little of their language, mostly signals that they send to one another. At first they were suspicious and scolded me, always chattering. Then I began to help them gather seeds and nuts and fruits.

"They carry their food in pockets that are near their cheeks and their faces get all puffed up. I think they were very surprised when I stuffed the food I gathered into the pockets of my skirt. After that, they treated me more like a chipmunk than a human."

"Oh my goodness!" exclaimed Granny Little. "What a brave and resourceful girl. You are, indeed, as amazing as Tom has told us. And your speech and grammar are excellent."

Tom leaned over toward Glory and whispered, "Granny loves books and, well — grammar. She doesn't want children using bad English when they speak or, especially, write. She doesn't care too much if we don't spell well as long as we all use, as she says, 'the principal requirements of plain English.' She's from — you know — the old days."

"I hope you will enjoy spending a little time with us before going home," said Mr. Little to Glory. "Cousin Dinky and Della, his wife, are out somewhere in the Big Valley

delivering mail — letters to tiny people all over the valley. Dinky won't be able to fly you to your home and family until they get back, in the next few days."

"Great!" said Tom. "We'll have fun. We can show Glory around the Biggs' house, right, Dad? Have you ever seen a regular-sized person, Glory? They're *huge*!! Almost as tall as that big bear we saw . . . and no tails, none — it's weird."

Uncle Pete, Tom and Lucy's other uncle, told Glory he would be glad to show her his stamp collection. "Been saving stamps since I was a boy," he said. Glory had no idea what a stamp collection was, but she listened carefully to everything Uncle Pete said and learned all about it.

Uncle Pete told everyone that Glory was "a quick study" and an exceptional child.

"Glory," said Lucy, "do you think I could ever get to take a ride on one of those tiny horses that you have on your farm?"

"Maybe, Lucy," said Glory. "Right now my father won't even allow *me* to take a ride. I hope he'll change his mind one day and see that girls can do many things just as well as boys. Anyway, if you come to our farm, you and I will sneak a ride on Gentle, my favorite. I promise."

Uncle Nick, who was listening, said, "I think a visit to Glory's farm may be possible after all. Cousin Dinky, the Big Valley's greatest airman, has been testing the balloon. The hot-air stove-pump is working just fine. Maybe he will rev it up and fly us all to the top of the mountain to meet Glory's family."

"Hooray!" yelled everyone.

And that's exactly what happened.

The next day, Cousin Dinky returned from his airmail duties. Della took Granny, Mrs. Little, and Baby Betsy in the glider. Everyone else climbed aboard the red balloon's basket. The wind was favorable, and in hardly any time Cousin Dinky made a perfect landing in the meadow next to the Nunsuch farm, on top of the steep mountain.

Mrs. Nunsuch came running from the house, Justice right behind her.

She had spotted Glory climbing out of the balloon.

"Glory! Glory! You're alive!"

Glory ran to meet them. "It was an accident, Mother," she said after hugging her. "I couldn't get home. The Littles saved me, especially Tom and Lucy and Uncle Nick."

She pointed them out.

The Little family crowded around, smiling and laughing.

"Where is Father?" asked Glory, looking about.

"Glory, your father was brokenhearted when you disappeared," said Mrs. Nunsuch. "It was the night of the big rainstorm, and afterward you were missing. We looked everywhere. I thought you had floated away and died in that awful storm.

"I knew you were playing on that raft at night. Your father thought you had run away because he treated you badly by not allowing you to do things you can do as well as Justice. He knows now that you should have been allowed to ride horses, climb trees, and ask questions if you wanted to. He has *changed*, Glory.

"He takes long rides on his horse and comes back very late, so he doesn't get enough sleep, and I'm worried that he might fall asleep in the saddle and hurt himself."

"Where is he now?" asked Glory.

"He went down the south road." Mrs. Nunsuch pointed. "It's been a long time. He should be coming back at any time now."

Glory ran to the barn and came out almost immediately, riding bareback on one of the tiny horses.

Not long after that the farmer and his daughter came back together, laughing and talking as their horses trotted across the field to the farmhouse.

THE LITTLES STAYED to help celebrate Glory's return. Lucy took a ride on a tiny horse with Glory. Mrs. Little had a long talk with Serenity Nunsuch about bringing up children. Baby Betsy spent time in Mrs. Nunsuch's lap. Mr. Little sketched them.

Mr. Nunsuch insisted that Cousin Dinky give him a short ride in the red balloon. Mr. Nunsuch got a bit airsick. "There's nothing like a horse," he said, "but I enjoyed it."

Grandpa Little told the Nunsuches that he would see to it that their excellent family and their neighbors, the Farm Tinies, would have a page in *The History of Tiny People*, written by Charleton Booker, the tiny historian of tiny people at the city library.

Uncle Pete, Uncle Nick, Della, and Dinky took a swim in the pond. (They had brought their bathing suits.)

Tom, Glory, Lucy, and Justice had a race to the apple tree and Glory came in far ahead. "She must have cheated," said Tom, laughing. "Girls can't beat boys in a race — besides, I stubbed my toe."

Mrs. Nunsuch prepared a late lunch:

The Menu
One Sweet Potato and an Apple Casserole
Sweetened with Butter and Honey

Goat Cheese Pancakes with Maple Syrup

Fresh Dandelion Greens

Yogurt Made with Goat's Milk and Served
in an Acorn Cup

Honey Cakes with Spices and Little Bits of Dried
Fruits and Nuts

Also, One Wild Strawberry Each

Cousin Dinky, the pilot who was also the family poet and songwriter, put his thoughts about Glory and the Littles into words and music that very afternoon.

Dinky wrote fine songs; everyone knew that. His problem was he sang off-key and didn't know it. He was such a fine person in every regard that no one could tell him. The only way his friends could stand his singing performances was to concentrate on the *words* of his songs, which were often thoughtful and worth listening to.

On this occasion Cousin Dinky got out his guitar (which he carried everywhere, just in case) and began to tune it, when the members of the Nunsuch family, to Dinky's surprise, brought out some musical instruments of their own and started tuning up. Mr. Nunsuch was on the banjo, Justice on the bass fiddle, Mrs. Nunsuch on the dulcimer, and Glory on the comb-and-tissue-paper, along with an occasional blow on the jug. "Looks

like we're going to have a hootenanny!"
yelled Dinky.

Dinky began strumming the guitar to the
tune he had written for the song, so that the
Nunsuch musicians could pick it up, which
they did in short order.

At first the notes from this strange band
were hesitant, jarring, and incomprehensible
to the listening Littles. But miraculously a
rousing good tune slowly emerged from the
band. Cousin Dinky began to sing.

Uncle Pete almost stuck his fingers in his
ears so as not to hear Dinky's terrible voice.
Luckily, he paused for a moment because, in
the midst of the irresistible playing of the
Nunsuches, Cousin Dinky found his voice.
For once he was singing in tune. This is the
song he sang:

Now —
    Glory was a lively child
    who never could be meek and mild.
    When she poured milk on the burning hay
    she never meant to disobey,
    but only saw what she could do
    and quick as a wink saw it through.
    Her swimming, running, and climbing skills
    sometimes gave her mother chills.
    But she was help in the kitchen, too.
    There wasn't much she couldn't do.
Sooo —
    All kids are born with talents inside them.
    Grown-ups can but love and guide them.
    Mr. Nunsuch declared this true,
    and saw at last what he must do.
    Amazing Glory must be free
    to be the best that she could be.

He'd teach her respect for horses and water
and still she could be a dutiful daughter.
And —
The Littles were happy to learn of friends
who live beyond where the valley ends.
They heard of the Farm Tinies' long, long
history.
It helped to solve many a mystery.
We know —
There's no one just like Glory Nunsuch.
From one tiny girl we learned so much.
All persons must be loved as they are.
Only then can they go far.
Only then can they go far.

Read more about the Littles' Big Adventures:

The Littles
The Littles to the Rescue
The Littles Take a Trip
The Littles Have a Wedding
The Littles Give a Party
The Littles and the Great Halloween Scare
The Littles and the Trash Tinies
The Littles Go Exploring
The Littles Go to School
The Littles and the Big Storm
The Littles and the Lost Children
The Littles and the Terrible Tiny Kid